The author would like to thank David J. Foster, Kris Kiler, Linda Berens, Kevin and Bradley Marcus, Kurt Wilberding, Sue Waterbury, JennyLeigh Tompson, Bob Self, Susi Talkington, Linda Sullivan, Phyllis Wender, Oliver Bode, Tricia Parks, Jennifer Hayes, Paul Toussaint, Lydia Christopher, Joel Stone, Laurel Graber, Margaret Bravo, Michael Gross at the Authors Guild, Todd Wenzel, Bill Robinson, and Quinn Gardner

Telos Publications
P.O. Box 4457, Huntington Beach, California 92605-4457
714.668.1818 or 866.416.8973 / fax 714.668.1100
www.telospublications.com

International Standard Book Number: 0–9664624–3-2

Cover/Book Design by Jenny Leigh Thompson & Visibility Designs
MBTI is a registered trademark of CPP Inc., Palo Alto, California.

Printed in Hong Kong

For my wonderful husband
David J. Foster
&
Bruce Talkington
the best teacher I ever had

with a *very* special thanks to
Sue Waterbury

Hi! My name is Tina Talkington,
and I can make my stuffed animals talk!

I have four cuddly stuffed animals.
Each one is very different, and I love them all.

This is Fox. He's always running really fast.
I love him because he's fun, and he has really big ears.

Beaver's different. He's very responsible. And he can build anything he wants with his funny, flat tail.

Owl is always thinking and thinking. She wants to know how everything in the world works, and she never stops reading.

Dolphin loves to play and dream.
She swims in my bathtub.
She thinks it's the ocean!
Dolphin is always telling me to be nice to
my little brother, even though sometimes
I don't like playing with him.

My little brother never leaves me alone. He's always throwing my animals around! But when I'm in my room, I can do magic spells that help me get away from my little brother. Watch this!!!

Alakazam Kazoo Kazive, make my animals come alive!
Alakazam Kazim Kazoo, shrink me down to toy size too!

"Oh, no!" cried Tina. "My little brother was hiding in my room, and my magic spell went wrong! Now my brother is an even bigger baby. And Dolphin should be in the sea, not the tree!"

"Hoooww did it happen?" Owl wanted to know.

Dolphin shrieked, "I remember Tina doing a magic spell. That's when you, and I, and Beaver and Fox came to life! Then there was a terrible outburst and there was a horrible GIANT! He was sniffling and crying and twirling me around until I landed in this tree. EEEEEE!!"

"Well," hummed Owl, "I know a lot about dolphins and,
I can tell you, I never heard of a dolphin up a tree."
Tina cried out, "We have to get Dolphin out of the tree!!
There is no water up a tree!"
"I suggest you try flying," puffed Owl. "It's much easier
than falling, and you won't break yourself."
"How do you fly?" asked Dolphin.
"You just flap your wings like this, see?"

"That's a great idea, Owl," said Tina. "Could I please pluck
out a few feathers?" she asked as she started pulling.
"Ouch!" Owl grumbled. "That hurts!"
"Hold still. I only need a few more," said Tina.

Tina stuck Owl's feathers into Dolphin's delicate skin.
"Now you can fly," said Tina.

Dolphin flapped her fins, but the feathers did not move.
She fell to the ground with a loud *kerplunk!*
"This will never work," said Dolphin.
Owl agreed, "Dolphins don't fly, and if you borrow any
more of my feathers, neither will I."

Owl turned to Fox. "Fox, we need to get Dolphin to
water before she dies. Will you help?"
"Why won't she walk like the rest of us?" asked Fox.
"Is she stupid?"

Fox sniffed Dolphin up and down. "She's dead. We can use her for a rug."
Owl hooted back, "She's not dead! She's lost! She's a fish out of water!"
"I'll settle this," said Fox. "I hear you are sick and you need to get to water?"
Dolphin let out an ear-piercing squeal. "I want to go home where I belong."
"Have you tried walking home?" asked Fox.
"How do you walk?" asked Dolphin.
"With your feet," Fox replied.
"But I don't have any feet," said Dolphin.

Fox fell to the ground laughing. "All you need to do is get Dolphin some shoes."

"You can wear my shoes," said Tina.

Fox grabbed the shoes and shoved them on Dolphin's fins.

"Problem solved. Now you can walk home."

Dolphin frowned as she tried to walk in the tiny shoes.
She flipped around until her fins collapsed under her.
"Oh boy, this really is a pathetic creature,"
Fox giggled. "I can't help such a silly fish."

"I'm not made to walk or fly, and I'm not a fish!
I'm a dolphin! I swim. I'm different from you.
Why can't you understand that?"
"Why can't you understand that walking is easy?"
snapped the Fox.
"Easy for you," cried Dolphin. "You have feet,
but I have fins."
Fox saw her fins for the first time. "I'm sorry, Dolphin,
I thought all animals had feet, and fur too."

Suddenly, there was a familiar banging noise.
The animals were terrified.
"Waaa! Waaa!" the Giant cried.
"Oh, no, the Giant is here again!" Fox howled.
Tina shouted, "Go away, you big baby."
She turned to the animals, "We have to hide
before the Giant gets us."
"I'll get Beaver to help," said Fox, racing off.

"Beaver! Beaver!" yelled Fox. "The Big Bad Giant is coming, and Dolphin's crashed on the ground. She can't fly, and she can't walk, but she can swim...*if*...we get her to water."

"Well, Fox, perhaps if Dolphin was more responsible and organized, she wouldn't be in this mess. Now, if you'll excuse me, I'm a very busy beaver, and I have to finish gnawing wood for the family den."

Then the banging and crashing started again, and the whole world shook!

"I miss the water, Tina," cried Dolphin. She slowly lowered her snout to the ground, and a huge tear fell out of her eye.

"Hurry," sniffed Fox. "I can smell the Giant. We're running out of time."

"Well, I've been doing some reading," Owl hooted. "It would seem that Dolphin is right. We are all very different, and she is not made to walk or fly, so I have a new plan. We need to build a giant nest to hide in."

"We need sticks!" Beaver said with confidence.
"We need glue and blocks, too! We need to
build a sturdy wooden wagon to hide in!"

Owl flew up to her perch. "I can see the
Giant coming. Beaver, please start building!"

"We're all going to have to work together," said Dolphin.

"That's right," said Beaver. "Everyone has to help."

Dolphin groaned as Beaver grabbed her tail and started using it as a shovel.

They slapped down the wagon roof as the Big Bad Giant charged closer. "I want to come in!" the Big Bad Giant screamed. "I want to play, too!"

The animals were terrified. They huddled together, shaking and shivering, almost too scared to breathe.

"Oh, no!" said Tina. "We have to get out of here fast!"

"We need to work as a team," said Dolphin. "Let's put our heads together. We need to build an idea—*together*!"

"I can put genuine wooden wheels on this wagon," said Beaver.

"I can fly above and draw a map," said Owl.

"I can run ahead and clear a path to the water," said Fox.

Beaver cheered, "Everybody, all together—*puuush!!!*"

As Tina and the animals saw the water ahead, they heard the Giant chasing after them.

"Waaaa, play with me! Play with me! Waaaa! Waaaa!" he cried.

"No!" shouted Tina. "We don't want a big baby in our group. You're too loud, and you're always throwing my animals around! Now go away!"

The Giant shouted back, "I'm not a baby. I'm two, and I'll help you push Dolphin to the water!"

For the first time, Tina listened to her little brother.

"Tina," said Dolphin warmly, "maybe the Big Bad Giant isn't so bad.
Maybe he's just different from us."
"Yes, and if we let your brother help, we could stop running from him," said Owl.
Fox jumped up and down, "Cool. It might be fun to play with him."
"That's true," Beaver added. "Besides, he could help us push Dolphin to the water."
"Yeah, maybe it would be fun if we all played together. But just for today," said Tina.

Tina's brother helped push Dolphin back to the ocean. Dolphin swam
laps around the other animals while she taught them the breaststroke.
They all splashed and played until bedtime.
"This is the best day I ever had," said Tina.
"The best!" they all said together.
Then Tina Talkington opened her magic spell book again.
She twirled around and said the magic words,

Alakazam Kazive Kazoy, turn my animals back to toys.
Alakazam Kazim Kazoo, turn me back to kid size too.

Wow! It worked! Making my animals talk is fun, especially when
I'm mad at my little brother. Playing with my brother is fun too.
Well...sometimes.

Telos Publications was founded in 1988 to promote the understanding and application of individual differences. The understanding of the four temperaments has been recorded for at least twenty-five centuries. Using the Keirseyan Temperament Theory, introduced in the popular book *Please Understand Me*, Kimberly Foster makes the understanding of individual differences accessible to children with *A Dolphin Up A Tree!*

For more information about ordering more copies or for continued interest in temperament theory, please visit our website at http://www.telospublications.com.

Magic Bridge
Theatre Company

Bring the magic to your school

Dear parents and teachers,

If you enjoyed reading this book perhaps you would like to bring the live musical to your school or community. We would love to hear from you. Please visit http://www.dolphinupatree.com for more information about how you can bring the magic to your school.

And if you or your child would like to talk with us or any of the characters in the book please feel free to e-mail us at magicbridge@fosterentertainment.net.

Kindest regards,

Kimberly Foster

333 West 52nd Street Suite 802 New York, NY 10019
v: 212 245-1014 f: 212 937-2229 magicbridge@fosterentertainment.net
www.dolphinupatree.com